CSJ
10/16

LIVING THE LIE

D1585929

B000 000 019 3912

ABERDEEN LIBRARIES

Titles in Teen Reads:

Badger Publishing Limited, Oldmedow Road, Hardwick Industrial Estate, King's Lynn PE30 4JJ
Telephone: 01438 791037

www.badgerlearning.co.uk

LIVING THE LIE

ANN EVANS

Living the Lie ISBN 978-1-78464-623-3

Text © Ann Evans 2016
Complete work © Badger Publishing Limited 2016

All rights reserved. No part of this publication may be
reproduced, stored in any form or by any means mechanical,
electronic, recording or otherwise without the prior permission
of the publisher.

The right of Ann Evans to be identified as author of this Work has
been asserted by her in accordance with the Copyright, Designs and
Patents Act 1988.

Publisher: Susan Ross
Senior Editor: Danny Pearson
Editorial Coordinator: Claire Morgan
Copyeditor: Cambridge Publishing Management
Designer: Bigtop Design Ltd
© redsnapper / Alamy Stock Photo

2 4 6 8 10 9 7 5 3 1

CHAPTER 1

SWEET LITTLE LIES

They say you can't fool all of the people all of the time. But I can. And I do.

Me and Kim, my best friend, walk home together every afternoon after school. Well, just to here, to the railway bridge. Then she goes her way. I go mine.

"See you tomorrow, Kim," I say, reminding her about the homework.

"See you, Ella!"

With a wave, I head towards the smart tree-lined avenue, looking like I might go into any one of the big posh houses at any second. I turn and wave. Kim waves back, and I walk on, school bag on my shoulder, long ponytail swishing.

I've been lying all my life. And I get away with it. Why tell the truth when you can fib? Anyway, that's what people would rather hear. They wouldn't *really* want to know the truth. So I keep the truth locked inside of me, and wrap a cloak of lies around myself every time I set foot outside my door.

I sneak one last look over my shoulder. Kim's gone. So I cross the road. Run down the entry between two big houses. Then I keep running. Eventually, I come out by the shops, then I cross the common towards the flats.

No one knows I tell lies. Not even the person these untruths are about — my mum. To my friends, my mum is a smart businesswoman. "Yes, she's a qualified freelance accountant," I tell them. "She's up to her eyes in work. She has so many clients."

Don't get me wrong, I don't like dishonesty. Only it has to be done. I couldn't tell anyone the truth — I just couldn't. The consequences would be too terrible. Disastrous.

And so I lie.

As ever, I feel my stomach tighten as I near home. I worry what I'll find.

There's rubbish dumped in the alleyways here. Old mattresses, bike wheels, broken pushchairs. I hurry on to the row of flats. Not high rise flats. These are just three levels.

I go down the pathway to the broken glass doors. There's a combination lock, only that's broken too. I've rang the landlord loads of times to try and get it fixed. He doesn't seem to care.

The smell of urine hits me as I go in. There's a scruffy drunk leaning on a flat door. "Kcy won't work," he slurs, his eyes baggy and bloodshot.

"That's because you don't live here," I tell him. I know most of the people living here. Even the druggies and drunks — like this one. I hold onto his arm, lead him outside and point him in the direction of the next block. "Your flat's over there!"

It hasn't always been just Mum and me. I had a dad until I was five. When he left, Mum said he'd got a new job which was miles away. He'd be back, one day.

She'd lied. He'd just decided he didn't love her — or me — anymore. So he'd left. Mum didn't tell me that. I worked it out for myself.

Mum did a lot of crying when I was five and six. Crying and moping around. Once, someone — I know now it was a social worker — took me away from Mum. Made me live with another family. I hated it. I missed her so much. There was a boy there who would pinch and kick me when no one was looking. I was so glad when the social worker said Mum was well enough to look after me again and I could go home.

She didn't cry then. She seemed happy. She drank a lot, though. She told me it was her special lemonade — and no, I couldn't have any. She bought me my own lemonade and we'd sit watching the TV at night, drinking our pop.

Of course, hers was vodka.

Sometimes she sat up drinking long after I went to bed. Then she didn't wake me in the morning and I'd be late for school. I heard the teachers talking about me. I heard those dreaded words — *social worker, foster home*.

I was eight. But I wasn't stupid. So I set the alarm clock every night. I got myself up early, got her up. Made us breakfast, combed her hair, helped her dress, ironed my school uniform.

One day my teacher said to me, "Ella, you're looking so smart these days. Is everything OK at home now?"

I smiled the brightest smile. Honestly, I'm sure I even made my eyes shine with joy. "Yes, thank you. And we're moving to a new house. Mum's got a new job as an accountant. Everything is wonderful!"

I was quite clearly a brilliant liar. Although one bit was true. We did move to a new place. Mum lost her job because she was never there. She couldn't pay the rent, so we moved to a crummy old flat. This one.

Mum gave up drinking. I'd nagged her so much. Every time I found a bottle of vodka, I poured it down the sink. The last time I did that, she went crazy. She just hit me and hit me. Then she crumpled sobbing to the floor, telling me how sorry she was.

That was a turning point. She went to the doctor.

To help her get off the booze, he put her on pills. That didn't work so he put her on more pills. She stopped drinking, only then she got really down and depressed. Our doc had the answer — more pills.

Sometimes, when I'm at school, she lets the neighbour in. Says she gets lonely. It scares me in case he gets her hooked on something else. Recently she's been trying to stop taking the pills.

"I'm sick of taking tablets, Ella," she'd said only last week. "I want to get myself sorted. No drugs, no alcohol. I'll get a job. We'll move somewhere nice."

I'd heard it all before.

Climbing to the third floor, I turn the key. My stomach has tied itself into a knot. Our flat isn't a dump, it's clean and tidy. I make sure of that.

"Mum! I'm home!"

I can hear someone talking. It's a deep, growling voice. A shiver runs up my spine. "Mum?"

She's in her chair, rocking back and forth. I look round, expecting to see someone else. There's no one. I check each room. I hear the growling voice again, and I dash into the living room.

The voice is coming from my mum. I go icy cold. "Mum, why are you talking like that?"

She looks at me, but her eyes seem odd, bulging.

"Mum, are you all right?"

"You can taste it, at the back of your throat."

"Has someone been in here today, Mum?"

She grabs my wrist, pushes her face close to mine. The veins are standing out on the back of her hands. "It's like metal." She sticks out her tongue, and she looks awful.

"I'll make you some tea," I say, easing her hand from my wrist. "Have you had any visitors today?"

She doesn't reply. It's like she's in another world. She's taken something, that's obvious. One of the neighbours has wormed his way in. Given her some drugs or booze, maybe both.

As the kettle comes to the boil, I peel potatoes and put a pie in the oven. This is the routine — I make dinner. Only today, I'm shaking inside. Partly with anger that someone's given her something. Partly because the way she's acting is frightening me.

It's quiet in the living room, and I look round the door. She's just rocking back and forth. Then she sees me and smiles.

It's not a normal smile. It's an awful, manic smile. Not Mum's smile at all. A thought strikes me. Is it possible to go insane overnight?

CHAPTER 2

KNOCKING ON DOORS

I try to get her to drink her tea and I tell her about my school day. I tell her what I've been studying. Tell her about Kim and my other friends. When the pie and veg are ready, I dish up our dinners. She picks at hers like there's something nasty in there, taking the lid of the pie off, and poking about with her fork.

"Mum, it's chicken and veg. We've had it before. It's nice."

She screws up her nose. "Tastes like metal."

"No, it doesn't."

Neither of us eat much. I'm aware of her all the time — rocking and muttering under her breath, pulling faces.

"So, who have you talked to today, Mum?" Someone must have been in and given her something. I'll kill whoever it was. After all the time it's taken her to get off drink, then someone messes with her head again.

I put the TV on, wanting life to be normal. Well, as normal as it can be for us. I find a quiz show. She likes quizzes. She says it's how she got her education, listening to the questions and answers. Only now she sits back in her chair, as if she doesn't like what she sees.

"What?" I ask.

"There's that metal noise. Hear it?"

"What is it with metal, Mum? The telly sounds fine."

"No, he heard it as well!"

"Who?"

She jabbed her fork at the screen. "The man. The quiz man. He just said there's metal. It'll get into your blood if you're not careful."

"He didn't say that. You're hearing things, Mum."

I push my plate aside and go looking for bottles or drugs. I check the drawers and cupboards, the rubbish. Checking her room, the only pills I find are the ones from the doctor.

I grab my door keys. "Will you be OK for a few minutes?"

"Where are you going, Ella?" she looks frightened, and my heart aches for her. So I go back to her chair and give her a hug. "I need to ask our neighbours something. I'll only be a few minutes."

"Don't be long."

I knock on the flat door opposite. The guy who opens it is a big six-foot lump of lard. A lager lout. I found him in our flat once. I'd come home from school early with stomach ache, and he'd been sat there. I'd yelled at him to get out. And when he didn't move, I'd pulled him by his jumper and pushed him out the door. All 20 stone of him. He's never let me forget it.

"Allo! Mighty Mouse. How's your Ma?"

He's a big fat lazy lump and I hate him. "Have you been in our flat today?"

"Nope, not me. I wouldn't dare. Not after the last time."

He's being sarcastic. "I'm serious. She's not herself. I want to know if you've given her anything?"

"Woah! No way! I don't do drugs. And your Ma doesn't like lager." He nods his greasy head at the flat door next to ours. "Ask him. He's been nosing about. Bit young for your Ma. Nice boyfriend for you, though."

The flat next to ours has been empty for weeks. I'd heard some homeless guy had moved in. Great. Another druggie or layabout. "What do you mean, nosing about?"

"He was knocking on your door today…"

"Was he!" I march across and bang on his door with my fist.

A boy of about 17 opens it. It takes me by surprise. He doesn't look rough or a druggie. He looks like a student. A nice-looking student. His cheeks dimple when he smiles. "Hi!"

I'm a bit thrown for a second. But only for a second. "I live there," I tell him, pointing at my door. "You were knocking my door today. Did my mother let you in?"

"No she didn't. I'm Ben, by the way."

My chest feels tight. I haven't time to stop and chat. "I don't care who you are. Why were you knocking our door?"

"I was just checking things were OK. There was a lot of noise."

My heart sinks. "What kind of noise?"

"Well, like a drawer banging shut. Like a knife drawer: *slam, clink, slam, clink*. For about an hour. It was odd, so I knocked. The noise stopped then."

"You'd better be telling the truth!" I warn him.

The big lump of lard is still there. He laughs. "She means it. She's only little but she packs a punch!"

I flash looks that would kill at both of them and go back indoors. Mum seems glad to see me.

"Here you are!"

I hug her, and take her plate away to wash up. Putting the clean cutlery away, I close the knife draw a bit too hard and listen to the sound. *Slam, clink*. Like he said.

Only why would Mum stand here, opening and shutting the drawer for an hour?

The worry keeps me awake half the night.

***

There is a shorter route to school. Only I take the path across the common, past the shops, up the entry, into the avenue of big houses. I slow down then. It's OK if I'm seen here.

I didn't want to leave Mum this morning. I checked that she'd taken her tablet, and she stuck out her tongue for me to see. I hadn't asked her to do that. It was horrible. She'd never acted like that before, even when drunk.

"Ella!"

Reaching the bridge, I hear Kim shouting. I wait for her to catch me up. My happy, carefree smile is already pasted across my face. "Hi!"

Her hair is like mine: long, worn in a ponytail.
We sit together in class. We get teased sometimes.
We get called the *brain box twins*. Only she's
naturally brainy. I cram my head full of stuff.
I have to work so hard to keep up.

If you get bad grades the teachers want to know
why. They start looking at your home life. Well,
no one is going to check my home life again. If
I get put into care, I dread to think what would
happen to Mum.

Kim falls into step with me. "Do you fancy
coming over to my house one night this week?
We could watch a film, eat popcorn."

We've been best mates since year seven but she's
never ever been to my place. That's never going
to happen. I've never been to hers either, even
though she's always asking me to. "Sounds good,"
I answer, as we merge with other kids going into
school. I point out the new colour of another
girl's hair. I'm pretty good at changing the subject.
Avoiding making promises I can't keep.

Today, it's harder to concentrate on my school work. All day I'm wondering if Mum is banging the drawers. And I'm scared she'll let someone in.

"So, how about tomorrow?" Kim says as we head to the science lab for the last lesson. But before I can come up with an excuse, she says, "And I'm not taking *no* for an answer."

I know she's on about going round to hers. She's always asking. I've used up every excuse in the book. But I need to be home. I need to check on Mum.

"I can't tomorrow…" I begin, but she cuts me off.

"It's OK. I'll save you from thinking up an excuse. Doesn't matter."

She sounds funny, like she's trying to stop herself from crying. "Kim?"

Then she blurts it all out. "You never come to my house. I know I'm not good enough for you. I know you live in a big posh house and your mum is the next best thing to Wonder Woman, but it would be nice to hang out together sometimes, out of school."

Her words stun me. "I'm sorry, I didn't think…"

Her eyes are shining with tears. "My family are just ordinary. Mum would love you to come for dinner. I'm always talking about you. But I know you'll always have an excuse."

"I'm sorry…" I murmur again. "It's not that I don't want to hang out with you. I'd love to, only…" I stop, on the verge of telling her.

But I can't. How can I tell her about my life? And admit to all these years of lying?

CHAPTER 3

OUT OF CONTROL

When telling lies is second nature, it's easy to come up with them. I make a decision. I'll nip home tomorrow lunchtime. I'll tell school I've a dentist appointment — just in case I'm late back — then I can check on Mum and make her a meal. I'd be able to go to Kim's house after school then. In fact, that would be great.

I put my arm around Kim's shoulder, and hug her. "I'm so sorry I've made you feel this way. I'm so selfish. I'd love to have dinner with you and your family tomorrow. It would be fantastic."

She blows her nose. "Ignore me. I'm stupid. If you've got things to do…"

"Nothing that can't wait," I tell her. "I'm sorry I can't invite you to my house. Mum's so… well, she'd drive you nuts!"

Kim's face lights up. "So you'll really come for dinner?"

It dawns on me then, how lucky I am to have such a good friend. We link arms, and for a few minutes I don't think about Mum at all.

***

I can't believe it! The combination lock on our flats has been fixed. I jab in the four numbers on the shiny pad, and the door opens. For a second I feel quite posh. The smell of urine has been swapped for the smell of bleach.

Things are looking up!

I run upstairs, turn the key and go in.

Mum's not alone.

"What are you doing here?"

Ben, the boy next door, is sitting on a kitchen chair, opposite Mum. She gives me a big smile. It's too wide and her lips are too red. And the veins in her hands are standing out too much again.

"Here's your daughter," Ben says to Mum, as if she can't see that for herself.

She rocks back and forth in her chair.

I kiss her forehead, and glare at Ben. "Mum, you shouldn't let strangers into the flat. I've told you that before!"

"Your mum's not feeling very well," Ben says gently, flashing unspoken messages at me with his blue eyes. "Maybe needs to see her doctor?"

"And you'd know that because…?"

"*Watch him…*" Mum's voicc is dccp and gravelly again. Her eyes narrow, suspicious.

"She'd like you to go," I warn him, keeping my voice soft.

"*Watch her…*" Mum's looking at me now.

"Is she on medication?" Ben asks.

"That has nothing to do with you!"

"You need to call your doctor."

"And you need to mind your own business."

"It's Ella, isn't it? Ella, look, I heard your mum shouting. I was worried…"

I'm not about to start discussing my mum with him. "Anyway, why aren't you at school? Or college? Or out looking for a job?"

"I am. I'm starting work as a painter and decorator. Learning the trade." He gets up, and walks to the door. To give him his due, he does look worried.

I follow him. Quietly I ask, "What do you mean — she was shouting?"

He takes a deep breath. "As if she was arguing with someone. But there was only one voice. Ella, is she taking her pills?"

"How do you know she's on pills?"

"I've seen this before. When someone's been on pills, then comes off them, the withdrawal symptoms can be bad."

I know he thinks she's a drug addict. "The only pills she takes are what the doctor gives her. So whatever you're thinking…"

"Just check that she's taking them." He gives me a little smile, which for some stupid reason makes me feel a bit wobbly inside. "I'm just next door if you need me."

"I won't!" I snap. "We don't need anyone."

Once he's gone, I try to act like everything is normal. I cook pasta and mince in a tomato sauce. But I can hear Mum muttering to herself.

It's not her voice. It's a horrible voice. It makes me shudder.

We eat on trays on our laps. I talk about all the usual stuff. I tell her about the flat door lock being fixed. I even talk about Ben and how he's got a job. She nods and she smiles. The tomato sauce is all around her mouth, and it makes her look odd, and frightening.

Not like Mum at all.

***

It's not as if she's old. She's only 41, and usually she cares how she looks. Going out isn't really her thing so I cut and style her hair. I choose her make-up and her clothes. But it's not like her to get food all around her face and not even realise.

I make a joke of it, pretending that it doesn't horrify me. I hand her some tissue. "Wipe your mouth, Mum. You're all tomatoey."

She wipes a bit off then drops the tissue on the floor.

I reach over to get it, before the tomato stains the carpet. Suddenly her fork is right before my eyes. Jabbed at me. I jump back before it prods me.

"Mum!"

"Don't touch me!"

My heart feels like it's jumped into my throat. "Don't jab me with the fork, Mum. Why did you do that?"

"Watching you!" she says in that voice again.

It feels like ice is running through my veins. "Mum… what's happening? You're not well. Are you taking your pills?"

"That's what you want, isn't it? Take my pills. Take an overdose. Kill myself!"

"No!" I cry, my heart breaking. I want to hug her. No, I want *her* to hug *me*. Only she's holding the fork, like a weapon. Or like something to defend herself with.

So I sit, trembling, not knowing what to do.

She's ill. She's mentally ill. She's falling apart before my eyes.

And so am I.

CHAPTER 4

SCARED!

The night seems endless. I can hear Mum muttering to herself. So many times I start to dial the doctor. Then stop. I'd be put through to the emergency doctor this time of night. And what would I tell them? That my mum's gone crazy? I can't do that to her. She's my mum.

There's no sound from her bedroom this morning. I shower and dress. Make breakfast for us both. I tap on her door and peek in. She's sitting on her bed, staring at her reflection in the mirror.

"Mum?"

She glances at me. "I'm looking old, Ella."

"No you're not," I say, crossing the room to sit by her. "You've just been a bit unwell. Are you feeling better today?"

"Tired. I couldn't sleep with all the music."

"Music?"

"It was too loud. Drums and things. Why do they play the music so loud?"

I hadn't heard anything. But Mum's room is at the front. "It might have been a car radio outside."

She smiles at me and pats my hand. "Be a good girl and tell them to be quiet."

I listen. There's not a sound. "Come and have breakfast, Mum. We'll put the telly on and listen to Breakfast TV. Have you taken your pills?"

She shuffles after me into the living room. We eat with the TV blaring. Then, while she's in the bathroom, I check her pills. Count them. I'll do this every day, then I'll know if she's taking them.

I hold out today's with a glass of water as she comes out of the bathroom. The suspicious look she gives me makes me want to cry.

"I've already had them," she tells me.

"Are you sure? I don't think you should just stop taking them."

"I've had them!" she shouts and dashes into the kitchen. Before I know it, she's pulled a pair of scissors from the drawer and is pointing them at me. "I'm not taking any more!"

"Mum! Put the scissors down!" I can't believe what she's doing. I turn icy cold. I feel sick.

But she doesn't put the scissors down. She takes them into the living room, sits down, and slides them down the side of her chair.

I'm too frightened to go near her — my own mum!

I need to ring the doctor, only I can't. I can't talk about how she's acting with her in the same room. And I'm scared. If she gets angry again…

Tears cloud my eyes. I try to pretend everything is OK. Like my own mum isn't scaring the life out of me.

"I'd… I'd better get off to school now. I'll pop back lunchtime because I have to go to my friend's house after school. Just for a while. So I'll be a bit late. Will you be OK?"

For a moment, she looks normal again. Like my mum. "That's fine, Ella. You have a nice time."

I grab my coat and school bag. "Bye."

"Bye bye, dear."

I close the door behind me, a lump in my throat. I stand there, listening. All I can hear is the TV.

No gravelly voice. No knife drawer opening and shutting. Maybe she's back to normal. But the memory of her with those scissors haunts me.

As I walk to school, I dial the doctor's number. Then hang up before it's answered. What do I say? My mum is acting weird. I think my mum has gone mad? And what if she points those scissors at someone else? What if she does more than just point them…?

No! She'd never hurt anyone.

The thought of my mum being a danger, a threat, shocks me. I dial the doctor's number again. Only this time it's answered before I can hang up.

"Hello. Doctors Lee and Hope surgery."

The words stick in my throat.

"Hello? Can I help you?"

"Oh, yes… hello. This is Ella Burrows. Eight Chapel End. Would… would it be possible for the doctor to see my mum?"

"I've no appointments today…"

"No, could he come and see her?"

"What's the problem?"

"She's… she's not herself and… and it's worrying me."

"In what way?"

I can't say I'm scared that she'll hurt someone. I just can't. She's my mum! "She's hearing things, and just acting odd."

"Does she have a temperature?"

"I don't think so."

"Can she walk? Is she able to get to the surgery?"

"Well… yes…"

"I can fit her in at surgery at ten tomorrow."

"Yes, OK then," I agree, wondering if I'll have to lie to Mum about where we're going.

At school, I tell my teacher that I've got a doctor's appointment tomorrow. I keep quiet about Mum.

Kim is sympathetic. "Poor you. Dentist this lunchtime, then the doc's tomorrow."

I shrug. "It's OK. Just a check-up today. And Mum's been nagging me to get a mole on my back looked at." The lies roll so easily off my tongue.

Kim frowns. "Are you worried about the mole?"

"No. I've had it since birth. Mum's a bit paranoid at times." There! Not a single fib — all true!

"So," Kim says, linking my arm. "We're having Thai spicy chicken with noodles for dinner."

"Sounds fab! I'm really looking forward to it."
I am too. But I can't stop thinking about Mum.
My imagination is running wild…

By lunchtime I'm feeling sick with nerves.
Reaching home, I listen outside of our flat door
before turning the key. Then I call out. "Hi,
Mum! I'm home."

She appears in the kitchen doorway, still in her
dressing gown and slippers.

"Not dressed yet?"

She doesn't move from the doorway. It's like she
doesn't want me to go in there.

"I thought we could have soup and rolls, and you
could microwave a dinner for yourself later…
What are you doing?"

I look over her shoulder. There's stuff all over the
worktops. All our cutlery — all lined up.

"Having a tidy up?" I ask, trying not to feel freaked out. She's got the knives all pointing inward like spokes in a wheel.

I brush past her, open the cupboard and take out a tin of soup. I talk non-stop, trying to sound normal. But I'm too scared to turn my back on her. I'm looking over my shoulder all the time. My body feels like ice. I'm terrified of my own mother!

The soup warms up, and I need a knife to butter the rolls.

"Sorry to spoil your pattern," I say, taking one. She doesn't stop me, but I feel shaky inside. My smile is fixed in place. "Soup's ready. Let's go through and eat."

She eats in silence, and every time I look at her, she's eyeing me suspiciously. "Mum..." I try. "Are you feeling OK? I'm worried about you."

"Everybody's worried," she says in a voice that isn't hers.

"Why are you talking like that?"

"Why are *you* talking like that?"

"Like what?" I ask and she repeats it, mocking me.

"Like what?"

I don't know her any more. She's become a different person. Panic wells up inside of me. I hate myself. Why hadn't I pushed for the doctor to come out today? I know I won't be able to get her to the surgery tomorrow.

I can't eat, so I take my soup into the kitchen and pour it away. The knives lie there like some weird demonic symbol. I put everything back in the drawer. Then change my mind. I gather up the sharp knives and wrap them in a bag. Checking she's not watching, I hide them at the very back of a cupboard.

"I have to go back to school now, Mum. Don't forget I'll be a bit late back…"

She's got the scissors in her hand. She's jabbing them into her bread roll. She stops, thinking I hadn't seen her, and slips them down the side of her chair. She picks up her spoon and smiles. A wide smile that isn't my mum's smile at all.

My heart is breaking.

CHAPTER 5

MORE LIES

Back at school, Kim is pleased to see me. I feel sick. I want so badly to talk to someone about my mum. But it's not normal to be scared of your own mother, is it? How could I tell anyone that?

Somehow, I get through the rest of the afternoon.

"I know it's stupid," Kim says, as we grab our coats at the end of the day. "But I'm so excited that you're coming back to my house."

"Me too! My stomach's all tied up in knots." That was true. That's my trick. Mix a little bit of truth in with the lies.

Her parents turn out to be really nice — and normal. I envy her, having a normal home life. I'd love that. But I keep my unhappiness locked inside. And pretend.

Her mum has cooked us a really tasty meal. There's apple crumble and cream for pudding, which is heavenly.

I wonder if Mum and I will ever sit down to a normal meal again.

We watch a film up in Kim's room. It's gone ten o'clock when that ends. "I'd better go home. I've had a brilliant evening, Kim. Thank you!"

"Me too! My dad will drive you home. I'll come too."

"There's no need…"

But Kim is already putting her shoes and coat on.

"We're ready, Dad!"

He smiles and gets his car keys as we come downstairs. My mind is working overtime. "I can walk, it's no trouble."

"No problem," he says. "All set?"

Kim sits in the back of the car with me. "Ella lives in Beech Tree Avenue. What number, Ella?"

"I'll show you," I say, changing the subject. "That Thai chicken was gorgeous! Your mum is such a good cook."

We talk about food all the way back to the avenue with the big houses in. I didn't even know it was called Beech Tree. "Just on the left by the entry. Thank you so much!"

Kim and I hug then I get out of the car. Her dad doesn't drive off. They wait — seeing me safely inside. "I always go in the back way," I say.

"Which is your house?"

"That one," I lie, pointing to the one on the right. "Bye, then. And thank you. It's been lovely."

They still don't drive off, so I walk down the entry, waving back to them. Once out of sight, I hide in the shadows until I hear them drive away.

Then I run.

Reaching the common it looks pitch black. There's no way I can walk across there in the dark. And Mum would have a fit if she knew I was out here on my own at this time of night. I stare into the blackness but just can't drum up the courage to go that way. So I take the long way round, through the streets.

There's a car behind me, crawling along. I quicken my step, glad to reach the shops even though there's a gang of lads hanging about on the corner. I walk past them, ignoring their comments. The car is still following me, so I run. I keep running until I turn into my street.

There's an ambulance outside our flats.

My heart's in my mouth! I race in. Run up the stairs. It's Mum, I know it. Unless — unless she's hurt someone with the scissors, or found the knives. For some reason I think of Ben. *Please, please don't let her have hurt him — or anyone!*

Our door is wide open.

Ben suddenly appears from our flat. He holds me. "She's OK, don't panic!"

"What's happened?" I cry, struggling free from his arms and dashing in. Mum's in a wheelchair with a blanket over her, about to be wheeled out. "Mum!"

She's white-faced and looks terrified. "Ella!"

A paramedic steps forward. "You're her daughter?"

"Yes. Why are you here? What's happened?" I ask.

"I called them," Ben says.

"Why?"

"Your mum needs help."

"And you need to mind your own business!"

The paramedic speaks kindly, cheerfully. "Mum's a bit confused, so we're taking her in. We'll get her checked out, see what the problem is. Is there anyone else here? Your dad?"

"No. It's just me and Mum…"

"And how old are you, Ella?"

"Fourteen…" I groan. Why hadn't I lied? Why hadn't I said 16? I know what's going to happen now. They'll put me in care.

"Do you want to come in the ambulance with your mum?"

I nod. Tears are stinging the backs of my eyes.

The paramedics carry the wheelchair down the stairs. At the bottom, I can't believe my eyes. Kim and her dad are standing there, looking shocked.

My legs buckle under me.

CHAPTER 6

COLD TURKEY

Ben must have been right behind me because he grabs me, so I don't fall. Kim and her dad stand gaping. She's got to be thinking of all the lies I've told her. She must hate me.

"We followed you," Kim says in a clipped voice. "Dad knows the people who live at that house where you said you lived. So we followed you. Is that your mum?"

I can't speak, so I just nod.

"What's happened to her?"

"I don't know. It's her head… her mind…"

Kim's dad smiles kindly. "Well she's in the right hands now. You go with her, Ella. Kim and I will follow. We'll be able to bring you back — and your mum, if they don't keep her in."

She's gone crazy, I want to shout. They'll lock her up and never let her out. But I can't say that about my mum.

Amazingly, Kim puts her arm around my shoulders as Mum is settled into the ambulance. I can't believe she still wants anything to do with me.

"Why didn't you tell me?" she asks softly. "Why cope with all this alone? I'm your friend. You could have told me."

"Sorry," I whisper. And suddenly I can't bear to keep my fears locked up. I blurt everything out. "Kim, I'm terrified they'll put me into care. Mum's gone insane. They'll split us up. I'll be put into care. She'll be all on her own. She can't cope on her own…"

"Nor can you!" says Kim. "And you don't have to. I'm here."

"And me," says Ben, standing close by.

As I get into the ambulance, I feel as if a huge weight has been lifted off me. Ben, Kim and her dad smile encouragingly as the ambulance doors close. I take Mum's hand. Her eyes are wide and frightened. "I'm here, Mum. It's all right."

But it wasn't all right.

They put her in the psychiatric ward. Take blood samples, examine her, ask questions — ask me questions. I tell them everything. There's no point in lying now. I feel awful talking about her this way. It feels so disloyal. She *is* my mum.

They give her something to make her sleep and tell me to go home. Kim and her dad have waited all this time. On the way home, I try to explain why I've had to lie. Try to explain how scared I am of being put into care because she isn't a fit mother. I tell them about before and about my dad, and my mum's years of drinking.

Kim listens, not interrupting. Finally, she says, "You poor thing. What an awful time you've had. But you don't have to face it all on your own now." She wraps her arms around me and I close my eyes, so glad to have a friend like her.

"Thank you," I say quietly.

Back in the flat I make hot chocolate for us all. Then a knock comes to the door.

It's Ben, looking worried. "Look, Ella, I'm sorry for poking my nose in…"

I feel so guilty suddenly. If Ben hadn't got involved, I dread to think what might have happened. I only hope he'll forgive me for being so nasty to him.

"Ben, I'm so sorry for what I said. I got you all wrong! I thought you were trouble. Out for what you could get. But you're really nice, and caring and…"

"Hey, you'll have me blushing!" he said, giving me a cheeky wink.

It makes me go a bit wobbly inside again. He really is nice. And he needs to know how thankful I am for 'sticking his nose in'.

"Honestly, Ben. I'm sorry for misjudging you. Mum did need help. And so did I. Thank you!" I don't know if it's OK to give him a hug, but I do anyway.

"Any time," he says, smiling. "So how is your mum?"

"She was sleeping when I left. Look, do you want to come in? I'm making hot chocolate."

"Sounds great!"

As he sits beside Kim's dad on the sofa, Kim gives me a wide-eyed look and mimes, "He's nice!"

For the first time in ages I find myself smiling. A real smile.

***

Mum's been in hospital for a week now. I visit every day. Sometimes Kim comes with me. She and Mum get along like a house on fire. The doctors and nurses are kind too, explaining why Mum went a bit *nutty* — which was Mum's word, not mine.

The doctor said that because she'd stopped taking her pills so suddenly, she got withdrawal symptoms. Hallucinating, becoming paranoid. The slang term is *cold turkey*.

The doctors are going to help her come off the pills — safely. It will take a while. And there'll probably be more times like this. Or depression might set in. But she's determined to do it. And at least I know there's help at hand if she does go a bit weird again. But I'm feeling really positive about it.

And today, Mum came home!

I've bought flowers and cake, and put up *Welcome Home* banners all around the flat. She's got a little plastic pill box with the days of the week on.

"Ella," she says, giving me a hug. "You have my permission to force feed me these things!"

We put our heads together and I hug her back.

"And I am so sorry for putting you through hell."

"It's OK," I tell her.

"I *will* get well," she promises. "I know I've said that before, but I messed up this time because I wanted to get off the pills straight away. But it doesn't work like that, does it, love?"

"No, it doesn't," I agree. "But now we know, we'll fight this together."

"Might not be easy. You know how down and

depressed I get at times."

"We'll face the problems as they come, Mum," I tell her.

"But not all on your own, Ella," she stresses. "And no more silly loyalty just because I'm your mum. If I go off the rails again, you tell them."

I smile at her determination, just as the doorbell goes. I have the sneaky suspicion that it's Ben.

But it's not. A woman is standing there. For a second I think it's one of the neighbours coming to check that mum's OK. But I don't recognise her.

"Hello?"

"Hello, dear. Is your mum home?"

She seems friendly. "Yes. Mum, you have a visitor."

"May I come in?" she asks.

I move aside, and she walks in. She smiles at me.
And then she shows me her ID card. I read the
words: *Mrs Paula Grey, Children's Social Care*.

The bottom falls out of my world.

CHAPTER 7

NO MORE LIES

My mind rushes back to when I was little. Someone just like her had come to see us. Then they took me away from my mum. They dragged me away, screaming and sobbing. Leaving Mum alone and crying.

Now it was about to happen again.

I couldn't bear it!

"I'm *not* going into care!" I shout, linking Mum's arm. "I don't care what your orders are. I'm not leaving here. I'm not leaving my mum…"

"It's Ella, isn't it?" she asks, trying to fool me with her kind smile. "No one is suggesting anything of the sort, dear."

"Then why are you here?"

"We had a referral from the hospital. It's routine. There's nothing to worry about. It's just my job to see how you're getting on. See if there's anything we can help you with. Basically, letting you know that we *are* here — if you need us."

Mum grasps what's going on before I do. "Ella, they're just letting you know that you aren't alone. Isn't that right, Mrs Grey?"

"Yes, indeed."

"Really?" I stare at her, wondering if she's lying. Trying to trick me.

"Yes, really. I understand how you feel, Ella. But I'm here to support you and help you. Not to split you and Mum up."

She's not lying. I can see it in her face. And in Mum's face.

My fears lift. Like a rain cloud that's been hanging over my head, it lifts and drifts away. The sun comes out. Whatever the future brings, I'll face it honestly. I have friends and my mum. And that's what matters.

No need for lies any more.

THE END

ABOUT THE AUTHOR

Ann Evans lives in Coventry in the West Midlands. She has written around 25 books including the award winning book, *The Beast*. One of her most recent titles is *Celeste*, a time slip thriller set in her home city. Her Teen Reads and Dark Reads titles are *Nightmare*, *By My Side*, *Red Handed*, *Straw Men*, *Kicked Into Touch* and *Living The Lie*. Ann also writes magazine articles on all kinds of topics.